JEWEL KINGDOM

The Ruby Princess Runs Away

D0980342

Jahnna N. Malcolm

THE WHITE WINTERLAND

THE VALLEY OF
THE DRAGONS

SECRET
CAVE

THE GREAT WALL

APPLESAP AND
MARIGOLD'S
COTTAGE

BUTTERCUP
MEADOW

JEWEL PALACE

THE RUBY
PALACE

BLUE
BONNET
FALLS

DEEP
DARK

THE RED
MOUNTAINS

RUSHING RIVER

THE SAPPHIRE
PALACE

BLUE LAKE

READ ALL THE

JEWEL KINGDOM

BOOKS!

#1: The Ruby Princess Runs Away

#2: The Sapphire Princess Meets a Monster

#3: The Emerald Princess Plays a Trick

#4: The Diamond Princess Saves the Day

JEWEL KINGDOM

The Ruby Princess Runs Away

by Jahnna N. Malcolm

Illustrations by Sumiti Collina

Scholastic Inc.

ISBN 978-1-338-61472-5

10 9 8 7 6 5 4 3 2 1   19 20 21 22 23

Printed in the U.S.A. 40
This edition first printing 2019
Book design by Maeve Norton

For Dash and Skye

The Shining Jewels in Our Lives

1

ROXANNE RUNS AWAY

"I can't do it," Roxanne whispered from her hiding place in the royalberry tree. "I can't be a Jewel Princess. I'm not ready."

Today was the day she and her cousins would be crowned in a coronation ceremony.

It was also the day they would leave the Jewel Palace, where they had grown up.

As the Ruby Princess, Roxanne would have to move to her new castle in the Red

Mountains. The mountains lay in the far corner of the Jewel Kingdom.

"I always knew this day would come," she murmured. "I just didn't think it would come so soon."

Roxanne stared glumly down at the palace courtyard. Creatures from every land were gathering there.

Nymphs with blue skin and green hair chatted with goat-footed fauns. Richly dressed lords and ladies bowed to pointy-eared elves who rode on the shoulders of smiling giants.

"There you are!" A little red bird with a rainbow plume on his head fluttered onto the limb next to Roxanne. It was Pip, the royal secretary.

"The king and queen have been looking for you everywhere!" Pip squawked.

Queen Gemma and King Regal ruled the
Jewel Kingdom. Today they were giving four
of the kingdom's lands to the princesses.

"Don't tell the king and queen where I am,
Pip," Roxanne pleaded. "I can't face them.
Not yet."

"The ceremony is about to begin." Pip
tapped Roxanne's hand with his long yellow
beak. "Everybody from the Jewel Kingdom
is here."

Roxanne's big brown eyes widened. "Everybody?"

"Everybody who's anybody." Pip ticked off the names of the guests on one wing. "There are the gnomes, the craghoppers, and the pixies from the Red Mountains."

Roxanne gulped.

"Then there are all those creatures from the Greenwood, Blue Lake, and the White Winterland."

Those were her cousins' lands.

"Then there are the young knights of Bronze, Silver, Iron, and—"

"Stop!" Roxanne pinched Pip's beak closed. "If you're trying to make me nervous," she whispered, "you are doing a very good job."

Pip shook his beak free from her grasp. He hopped to the limb above Roxanne's head.

"You shouldn't be nervous," Pip said. "You should be excited, like your cousins."

Roxanne's cousin Emily had been up since dawn, chattering about being crowned the Emerald Princess.

Demetra, the Diamond Princess, had spent the entire week in front of her mirror nervously brushing and brushing her shiny black hair.

Sabrina, the Sapphire Princess, was usually the quietest of the four. But even she had rattled on about sprites and striders and all of the new friends she would make at Blue Lake.

Every princess but Roxanne was happy.

"I just don't feel like a princess," she said with a huge sigh. "In fact, I feel very ordinary."

"Careful!" Pip glanced nervously at the palace windows. "Someone might hear you."

"But, Pip, look at me." Roxanne stood up in the crook of the tree. "I'm just a regular girl. I like to climb trees, ride horses, and go swimming."

"That will change," Pip murmured.

"I don't like dresses." Roxanne gestured to her beautiful red-velvet gown. "I'd rather wear pants."

Pip winced. "Heaven forbid."

"And how can I rule and protect the people of the Red Mountains when I can't protect myself?"

Roxanne showed Pip her leg. Her stockings were torn. And a very large lump had formed on her shin. "I banged my knee on the palace wall when I climbed up here."

Pip fluttered in circles around the tree. "Oh dear, oh dear!"

Roxanne tilted her head. "How does a person rule, anyway?"

"How should I know?" Pip ruffled his feathers. "You just order people around."

"Order people around." Roxanne wrinkled her nose. "That doesn't sound like fun."

"Who said being a princess was fun?" Pip squawked.

Ta-ra ta-ra ta-ra!

The trumpets sounded at the front gate. The palace guard announced, "Presenting the great wizard Gallivant!"

"Gallivant!" Roxanne gasped, nearly falling out of the tree.

The wizard was very old and very powerful. Just hearing his name made Roxanne weak in the knees.

"There he is." Below her, Roxanne could see the big white plumes of the horses that pulled the wizard's gleaming glass coach.

Pip flew to a ledge in the courtyard to get a closer look. He called to the princess, "Gallivant is carrying the Great Jeweled Crown!"

The crown held the royal jewels of the kingdom. Four jewels from this crown would be given to the princesses today.

Roxanne watched everyone in the court-yard bow low as the wizard passed.

"Soon they'll be bowing to me," Roxanne murmured. "I'll be in a coach with the Ruby Crown on my head. The coach will take me far away from my family and friends. And there I'll sit all by myself in some lonely old castle . . ."

Roxanne's voice trailed off. The palace gates were standing wide open.

Her eyes widened. *I don't have to be crowned today,* she thought. *I could just leap out of this tree and run away.*

Pip flew back to her. "Hurry, my lady. You must join the king and queen and your cousins. They're about to greet the wizard."

Ta-ra ta-ra ta-ra!

The trumpets sounded again.

"It's now or never," Roxanne said, keeping her eyes fixed on the open gate.

Queen Gemma and King Regal stepped onto the marble steps of the palace. A cheer rang from every creature in the courtyard.

Roxanne gathered her skirts around her, took a deep breath, and leaped. "Now!"

2

STRANGERS ON THE ROAD

"Princess, stop!" Pip cried.

He flapped his wings, trying to keep up with Roxanne as she raced down the mountain. "You must come back to the palace!"

Roxanne ignored Pip. She was too busy trying to run and put on her cape. She had grabbed the cape from one of the ladies-in-waiting as she raced through the palace gates.

"If you won't come back, then I'm coming

with you!" Pip declared, flying in front of her.

"Suit yourself," Roxanne huffed. "But I want you to know that I won't be going back. I'm through with being a princess."

"Do you know where you're headed?" Pip asked. "I mean, after all, you've never been far from the palace before."

Pip was right. Roxanne had only left the grounds twice. Once, when she and her cousins visited Gallivant's Cave. And another time on a butterfly-watching trip with Queen Gemma.

"I've seen maps!" Roxanne declared. She pointed to a glistening ribbon of water that ran across the fields in front of them. "I know that's the Rushing River."

"It moves very fast and is often difficult to cross," Pip said.

Roxanne pointed to a gloomy stand of trees. It crept across the pastures like a big dark shadow. "That is the Mysterious Forest."

"Oooh." Pip shuddered. "You want to stay away from there."

"Why?" Roxanne asked. "I've always been

warned to keep away from the Mysterious Forest but no one has ever told me why."

"Because . . ." Pip landed on her shoulder and whispered into her ear. "Because there is a secret passage in there. It leads straight to Castle Dread."

Roxanne's eyes widened. "Across the Dismal Sea? Where Lord Bleak and the evil Dreadlings were sent?"

Pip nodded.

Roxanne had often heard terrible stories of Lord Bleak. He had once ruled the Jewel Kingdom. But that was in the Sad Times, before Roxanne was born.

"Then I don't think we really need to go in the Mysterious Forest," she said in a shaky voice. "I say we head west."

"West is good," Pip said, glancing nervously

back toward the dark woods. He wanted to get as far away from them as possible.

Roxanne walked toward the Rushing River. "There should be a stone bridge just over that rise. I remember it from the maps in King Regal's study. We can cross the river there."

But as they reached the bridge, two figures in hooded black capes suddenly emerged from beneath it. They carried walking sticks and their hoods covered their faces.

"Who are you and where are you going?" one of them asked in a crackly voice.

A chill ran down Roxanne's spine. She pulled her cape shut to hide her fancy red dress.

"That's none of your business!" Pip squawked from his perch on her shoulder.

"What an unusual creature," the other cloaked figure rasped. It stretched one bony finger toward Pip. "The rainbow plume. Aren't those the palace colors?"

"Yes," Roxanne said quickly. "We're on our way to the coronation."

"Oh, really?" The other stranger hobbled forward. "But the palace is behind you."

"Excuse me." Pip pecked at Roxanne's shoulder. "*Excuse* me!"

She raised her hand to swat at the bird. "Pip, please stop that!"

The hooded figures gasped. Roxanne realized they were staring at her gown.

One hissed to the other, "The Ruby Princess!"

Pip tugged Roxanne away from them. "Th-th-these strangers," the bird stammered. "I think they may be D-d-dread— *Awk!*"

His voice was cut off as a third stranger
appeared from the woods and grabbed him.

"You let go of that bird!" Roxanne ordered.

"Come and get him," the figure whispered.

"Run!" Pip coughed. "Run!"

Before Roxanne could make a move, a
black shadow darkened the sky above them.

Roxanne looked up.

A huge green creature with red scaly

wings swooped toward her. It was breathing fire.

"By the Great Jeweled Crown," Roxanne cried as the creature plucked her off the ground with its claws. "A dragon!"

3

HAPGOOD THE DRAGON

"Permit me to introduce myself," the dragon said when they were far away from the hooded creatures. He gently placed Roxanne on the ground. "My name is Hapgood."

Roxanne was still a little rattled from the quick flight through the air. "Hapgood?"

The big green dragon nodded. He tucked his wings into his body and blinked his enormous dark blue eyes.

"But you may call me Happy," he said in a very deep, very formal voice.

"My name is—" Roxanne's hand flew to her mouth. She couldn't tell this dragon who she really was: Roxanne the runaway princess.

But she didn't want to lie to him, either. After all, he'd just rescued her from the hooded strangers. So she said, "I am Roxanne. Of the Rushing River."

The dragon held out one claw. She shook it—carefully.

"Pleased to meet you, Roxanne," Hapgood said. Then he added, "Of the Rushing River."

Roxanne couldn't help staring at the marvelous creature.

"I've only met one dragon before," she explained. "He was very fierce and spent a lot of time breathing fire. He burned up

trees and chairs—anything made of wood. Are you fierce?"

"I can be fierce when I want to be. But only when I meet creatures I don't like."

Roxanne looked back toward the bridge where the hooded strangers had tried to grab her. "I didn't like them at all."

Hapgood's smile vanished, and his eyes glowed red. "Those were Dreadlings. Sent by Lord Bleak. It's a bad sign when they appear in our kingdom."

"I wonder if King Regal knows about them," Roxanne murmured.

"Roxanne!" Pip squawked above them.

The little red bird was out of breath. His feathers were ruffled. One of his rainbow plumes was bent.

He fluttered onto a limb beside Roxanne's head. "I thought you'd been kidnapped!"

"No, Pip!" Roxanne laughed. "I'm quite safe. Meet Hapgood."

Pip turned up his beak at the big green dragon. "We've met." He sniffed. "He nearly burned off half my feathers with that flame of his."

Hapgood bowed his head. "Please accept my apologies. I was aiming for the Dreadlings."

Pip's little black eyes widened. "I knew they were Dreadlings. Oh, this is not good. Not good at all."

Suddenly, the ground beneath them began to tremble. The sound of hoofbeats filled the air.

Roxanne looked up to see a man wearing the rainbow colors of the Jewel Palace galloping toward them.

"It's Armstrong, captain of the palace guards!" Roxanne cried.

He'll recognize me for sure, she thought.

"Hide me!" she pleaded, darting behind the dragon.

"Why? What have you done?" Hapgood asked.

Roxanne bit her lip, trying to think of something. "I, um ... er, I ..."

"She stole a banner from the palace courtyard," Pip cut in quickly. "She wanted to have a souvenir of the coronation."

Hapgood pulled a red-and-silver shield from under his wing. "Put this on your arm. It will make you and anyone you touch invisible."

Roxanne didn't ask any questions. She quickly strapped the shield to her arm. Then Pip hopped onto her shoulder. Hapgood whispered the magic words.

"Magic shield with power so bright, hide them from all others' sight."

Roxanne and Pip disappeared from view.

"You there, dragon!" Armstrong called, pulling his horse to a stop. "The Ruby Princess has disappeared from the palace grounds. She was dressed all in red. Have you seen her come this way?"

Roxanne squeezed her eyes shut tight.

Did Hapgood see my dress? she wondered. *If he did, he'll know I'm the Ruby Princess.*

"No one has passed by me," Hapgood replied. "Do you think the princess was kidnapped?"

"The queen and king are certain of it," the captain said. "Queen Gemma is beside herself with worry."

Roxanne felt guilty. She hadn't meant to upset the king and queen.

"I think I saw a young girl in red clothes fishing by the stone bridge," Hapgood said.

"Thank you for that," Armstrong barked. "I'll check the bridge."

Holding her breath, Roxanne listened to the fading sound of hoofbeats as the guard galloped away. Then she removed the shield and reappeared.

"It really works," she gasped to the dragon. "The captain didn't see me or Pip."

"No, he didn't," Hapgood replied. "But it wouldn't have mattered. He was looking for the Ruby Princess. And you aren't the Ruby Princess." He put his face right up to hers. "*Are* you?"

Roxanne swallowed hard. "No. I have not been crowned the Ruby Princess," she declared straight to Hapgood's face. "I am Roxanne of the Running River."

"Didn't you say, *Rushing* River?" Hapgood asked, raising one eyebrow.

"I mean, the Rushing River," Roxanne said quickly. "I'm just a little nervous right now."

"Well, the captain has gone to look for the princess at the river's edge," Pip pointed out. "You don't have to worry about him."

"Hopefully, he'll see the Dreadlings and tell the king about them," Roxanne murmured to Pip.

She handed the magic shield back to Hapgood. "Thank you for the use of this wonderful shield."

Hapgood held up one claw. "Keep it. You may need it again. Remember, it has the power to make you invisible—but only for a short time."

"Someone's coming!" Pip squawked. "Put on the shield."

Roxanne spun around as two squat figures hobbled toward them.

One was a little woman with fuzzy red hair and a round face. The other was a tiny man with a long gray beard. He was limping.

"Are they Dreadlings?" Roxanne asked Hapgood.

The dragon shook his head. "These are gnomish folk from the Red Mountains."

He frowned. "And they appear to be in trouble!"

4

APPLESAP AND MARIGOLD

"My name is Applesap," the little bearded gnome said. "And this is my wife, Marigold."

"We need help," Marigold cried. "We've been attacked."

"You're hurt!" Roxanne cried, kneeling beside the little man. "Your leg has a bad gash on it."

Roxanne tore a strip of white cotton from her petticoat and handed it to Pip. "Take this to the Rushing River. Dip it in the water and hurry back."

"Right away!" Pip flapped off as fast as his wings would carry him.

Marigold had a scarf tied over her flaming-red hair. Her cheeks were dirty and streaked with tears.

"They came out of nowhere," she cried,

burying her face in her hands. "And took everything we had."

"Who did this?" Hapgood boomed.

"Dreadlings," Applesap moaned.

"They're terrible creatures," Marigold said with a shiver. "Just terrible." She put her arm around her husband's shoulder and cried. "Poor Applesap."

Roxanne frowned. "Does your leg hurt much?"

"It's not my leg," Applesap said, slumping down on a rock by the side of the road.

"It's his heart," Marigold murmured. "It's broken."

"You see, I'm a goldsmith," Applesap explained. "I was given the great honor of forging the crown for the princess of the Red Mountains."

"The Ruby Princess?" Pip asked as he returned with the wet cloth.

Applesap nodded miserably. "I was giving it to the great wizard Gallivant. He was to place the ruby in it and crown our princess."

Roxanne's heart went out to the little gnome. "Dear Mr. Applesap," she said as she gently cleaned his wound with the wet cloth. "You can make another crown, just as nice as the first one."

"And I can fly you to the Jewel Palace," Hapgood offered.

"But I can't go to the palace empty-handed," Applesap said. "What would the princess think?"

"She would think you were a very sweet man who's had an awful experience,"

Roxanne replied. "And she would invite you to have a nice cup of wildroot tea with her."

Applesap laughed. "I wish."

"But you don't have to worry about that," Pip cut in. "The princess has disappeared. Run away."

Marigold shook her head. "That's not true. We saw the princess crossing Buttercup Meadow."

"What?!" Roxanne and Pip gasped.

"Marigold's right," Applesap said. "The princess was traveling in a beautiful glass coach. She was dressed all in red."

Marigold pointed to the hem of Roxanne's dress peeking out from under her cloak. "Like your dress there, miss."

Roxanne leaped to her feet. "Are you sure about this?"

"Cross my heart," Marigold said.

"I even heard a knight in coal-black armor cry, 'Make way for the Ruby Princess!'" Applesap said.

Roxanne turned to Hapgood. "We have to go to the palace right now."

"But why?" Hapgood asked.

Roxanne tilted her chin high and declared, "Because that princess is an impostor!"

5

IMPOSTOR ON THE THRONE!

Roxanne stared at the dragon and the two little gnomes. None of them had moved a muscle.

"Didn't you hear what I said?" she repeated. "That princess is not a real princess."

"How—how do *you* know that?" Marigold asked.

"Because ... because ..." Roxanne turned to Pip for help.

"Because she is a friend of the princess's," Pip explained quickly.

"That's right." Roxanne nodded. "We're the best of friends."

"And," Pip continued, "she *knows* that the princess ran away."

Applesap squinted one eye shut. "But why would the princess want to run away?"

Roxanne took a deep breath. "You see ... the princess told me she doesn't feel ready to rule a whole land. She doesn't know how."

Marigold and Applesap looked at each other and back at Roxanne.

"But I thought she was trained for that sort of thing," Applesap said.

"She was." Roxanne tore another strip of cloth from her petticoat as she explained, "The princess had her own teacher. They studied the Sad Times."

"Ah, yes." Hapgood nodded. "When Lord Bleak and the Dreadlings ruled our kingdom."

Roxanne tied the bandage tightly around Applesap's leg. "The princess learned geography and science, too. She studied the kingdom's lands and the creatures that live in them."

"Did she learn to dance?" Marigold asked. "I love dancing."

"Oh yes!" Roxanne giggled. "And how to sing, too."

"How nice." Marigold nodded pleasantly.

"She studied math, and different languages, and the way the world works," Roxanne finished. "But no one taught her how to rule."

Marigold shrugged. "If you ask me, ruling is very simple."

"All we ask is that our princess have a keen ear and a kind heart," Applesap said.

"So that she might hear our problems and help us solve them," Marigold added.

"That's all?" Roxanne asked. "That just sounds like being a friend."

Marigold and Applesap smiled.

"That's right," Marigold said. "We would like the Ruby Princess to be our friend."

Roxanne looked confused. "But that's easy."

"For some," Hapgood observed. "But not for everyone."

Pip fluttered anxiously overhead.

"I hate to break up this tea party," he cut in. "But someone *must* go to the palace. We have to stop them from crowning the wrong princess."

"I'll go!" Hapgood cried, rising up on his hind legs. "And I'll take all of you with me. Hop on my back."

Marigold helped Applesap to his feet. The two gnomes climbed carefully onto the dragon's shoulders.

Roxanne frowned. "There really isn't room for all three of us."

"Then I'll stay," Applesap declared. "And you go. My leg feels much better, thanks to you."

Roxanne was torn. She knew she should go to the palace immediately. But Applesap was hurt. They couldn't leave him on the road. What if the Dreadlings came back?

"Applesap, you're hurt," Roxanne finally said. "You should ride. And, Marigold, you should go with your husband. I can follow on foot."

"Then I'll travel with you," Pip said, hopping off Hapgood's neck.

"I'll take Applesap and Marigold to the palace," the dragon said. "But how can we stop the coronation?"

"You don't need to stop it," Roxanne said. "Just delay it. I'll bring proof that she's a fake."

"We'll do our best." Hapgood unfolded his

mighty red wings. "Be careful, Lady Roxanne of the Rushing River."

Roxanne placed one hand over her heart. "I'll be very careful."

With a swoosh, Hapgood rose into the air. "And if anything unpleasant happens, use the magic shield."

Roxanne waved at the gnomes clinging to the dragon's neck. "I'll see you both at the Jewel Palace."

Hapgood wheeled in a circle and ordered, "Take the shortcut. You'll save time."

"Where is it?" Pip called.

The dragon boomed a reply that Roxanne did not want to hear.

"Through the Mysterious Forest!"

6

THE MYSTERIOUS FOREST

Roxanne and Pip followed a winding path deep into the Mysterious Forest. It was darker and colder than Roxanne had imagined.

"Pip?" Roxanne whispered.

"Yes, Princess?" Pip whispered back. He was riding on her shoulder.

"I'm scared."

"If it makes you feel any better," Pip replied, "so am I. Look." He held up one red wing. "All of my feathers are shaking."

The trees in the forest were twisted. The bushes were covered with long thorns. The smell of rotting leaves hung in the air.

A thorny branch reached out and tore Roxanne's skirt.

"Help!" Roxanne squeaked. "That bush tried to grab me."

"I wish we'd taken the long route," Pip muttered. "I don't like this place one bit. It feels evil."

"It is," Roxanne said with a gulp. "You said there is a secret path here that leads directly to Castle Dread. But where is it?"

"I don't know. That's why it's called a secret path." Pip pecked Roxanne on the top of the head. "Walk faster, would you?"

Roxanne tried to go faster. But every step was hard. Thick roots tripped her feet.

Tangled vines dropped from above and pulled at her hair.

Suddenly, she stopped dead.

"What is it?" Pip asked. "Why are we stopping?"

"Voices," Roxanne whispered. "I hear voices. Just around the blackthorn bush."

"I'll go see." Pip left Roxanne's shoulder. He flew to the bend in the path.

All of Pip's feathers stood on end. He opened his beak, but no sound came out.

"What is it, Pip?" Roxanne whispered, creeping up beside him.

"Those Dreadlings!" he croaked. "The three from the bridge. They're camped ahead. Turn back!"

"We can't, Pip. We have to get to the palace."

"But the Dreadlings," Pip cried. "They'll stop us."

Roxanne remembered the shield Hapgood had given her. "Not if they can't see us."

"What do you mean?" Pip asked with a puzzled look on his face.

Roxanne held up the shield and smiled. "We'll hide, Pip. Hop on my shoulder. We'll be invisible."

Once Pip was on her shoulder, Roxanne held the shield in front of her and murmured the words Hapgood had taught her:

"Magic shield with power so bright,
Hide us from all others' sight."

"Now let's go," she whispered.

Pip tapped her cheek. "Be careful, Princess."

Three Dreadlings in black capes were huddled around a map.

Roxanne started to tiptoe past, but something they said stopped her.

"Our plan is working perfectly," the leader said in a deep voice.

"Can you believe our good luck?" the shortest one snorted. "We were supposed to kidnap Princess Roxanne, but she saved us the trouble by running away."

The third one laughed hoarsely. "With the

real Roxanne out of the way, we can put our own princess on the throne."

"Our princess is already at the palace. I sent the carriage there myself," the shortest Dreadling declared.

"Have you taken care of the shape-changing mask?" the leader asked.

"Yes, Princess Rudgrin is wearing it. She is now Roxanne's mirror image."

"Rudgrin?" Roxanne whispered to Pip. "Isn't she the daughter of Lord Bleak? I thought she and her father were banished from our kingdom forever."

"They were," Pip replied. "And the evil Dreadlings were, too. But it looks like they're back."

"With Rudgrin securely on the throne in the Red Mountains," the Dreadling leader said, "we can then replace the other Jewel princesses, one by one."

Roxanne's eyes widened. "They are planning to take over the Jewel Kingdom!"

"Oh dear! Oh dear! We have to keep them from leaving the forest," Pip fretted. "But how?"

Roxanne looked around the Dreadlings' campsite.

Two giant roothogs and a gray-winged gorax were tied at the edge of the clearing. The roothogs were pulling up the roots of some blackthorn bushes with their tusks.

"I've got an idea," Roxanne said.

"What is it?"

"Those two roothogs and that gorax must be their rides," Roxanne whispered. "If we can tie the bird and the hogs to one another, then we can stall the Dreadlings."

"And that will give us enough time to run to the palace for help," Pip whispered.

"Exactly," Roxanne replied. "But we better hurry. I don't know how long this shield will hide us."

Roxanne slipped as silently as she could through the thick brush, grabbing a rope from beside the Dreadlings.

She tied the first roothog's reins to the other roothog.

Then she made a large loop and swung that over the gorax's head.

Grrawk! The bird shrieked as the rope tightened around its neck.

Roxanne froze.

"What was that?" The tallest Dreadling spun to look at the bird.

For the first time, Roxanne got a glimpse of a Dreadling's face.

She was surprised at what she saw. His face was absolutely normal. But his eyes were frightening. Two lifeless holes that looked like shiny black stones.

Roxanne shivered. What if the Dreadlings really did take over the Jewel Kingdom? They would make it a horrible place to live. And it would be all her fault!

"I won't let that happen!" she declared to herself.

"What's that?" the leader asked the other Dreadlings. "Did one of you speak?"

"It must have been the gorax," the short Dreadling replied. "She hasn't been the same since we crossed the Dismal Sea."

"Back to our plan," the leader said, rolling up the map. "With Rudgrin safely on the throne, there is only one thing left to do: find the real Ruby Princess and take her back to Castle Dread."

"Never!" Roxanne blurted out.

The Dreadlings turned just as the shield's magic wore off.

"Well, look who's here!" the leader hissed. "We're in luck!"

"Pip," Roxanne cried. "We're no longer invisible!"

"Run!"

7

FLY TO THE PALACE!

"Seize her!"

Two Dreadlings lunged for Roxanne. She fell backward into the gray-winged gorax.

"Pip!" Roxanne cried. "I have an idea."

She leaped onto the gorax and nudged its sides with her heels.

"Fly!" she ordered.

The gorax croaked. With a heavy flapping of its gray wings, it lifted her off the ground.

"Stop!" the Dreadlings shrieked, leaping onto the roothogs.

"The bird is tied to the roothogs," Pip cried. "It's lifting them off the ground!"

"Higher!" Roxanne urged the gorax. The great bird dragged the hogs and riders into the top branches of a tree.

"They're all tangled up!" Pip reported with glee.

"Cut the rope!" Roxanne ordered. "Or we'll be pulled back down."

"Leave it to me!" With a sharp *rat-a-tat* of his beak, Pip sliced the rope in two.

"Yes!" Roxanne cried as the gorax flew out of the trees. She prodded the gorax with her heels and commanded, "To the palace!"

"Well done!" Pip cheered as they swooped out of the Mysterious Forest and flew toward the palace.

Roxanne wanted to smile. But she couldn't.

"We can't celebrate yet, Pip. We still have to stop Rudgrin!"

When they reached the palace gates, Roxanne saw two tiny figures waving frantically.

"It's Applesap and Marigold!" she shouted. "Down, gorax!"

The beast obediently glided to a halt near the waiting gnomes.

"Thank heavens you're here," Applesap cried as he limped forward. "Marigold and I tried to delay the crowning but they wouldn't listen to us."

"We told them about the Dreadlings stealing our crown," Marigold wailed. "But they insisted they already had the crown."

"And they do!" Applesap said. "The one the Dreadlings stole from me."

"Where's Hapgood?" Roxanne asked.

"He went back to look for you," Marigold said.

Ta-ra ta-ra ta-ra!

"Trumpets!" Pip gasped. "They signal the coronation of the princesses. Oh no! We're too late!"

"Not if I have anything to say about it!"

Roxanne leaped off the gorax and dashed up the palace steps.

When she reached the throne room, Roxanne clasped the jeweled door handles with both hands and took a deep breath. "Here goes!"

She threw open the doors. The great wizard Gallivant had already crowned Roxanne's three cousins. Now he was

presenting the Ruby Crown to Princess Rudgrin.

Roxanne's velvet gown was torn. Her hair was tangled with blackthorns. But she knew who she was and announced it in a loud, clear voice.

"I am Princess Roxanne, the Ruby Princess of the Jewel Kingdom, ruler of the Red Mountains," she cried. "And I command you to *stop*!"

8

A Princess at Last

The Emerald Princess, the Sapphire Princess, and the Diamond Princess turned and stared.

Friends and family from all four kingdoms, including the young knights, stared.

Even King Regal and Queen Gemma were staring.

First at Roxanne. Then at the girl who sat on the throne.

"They're identical!" Queen Gemma cried.

"That girl is an impostor!" Roxanne declared. "Her name is Rudgrin. She's the daughter of Lord Bleak from Castle Dread."

Princess Sabrina and Princess Emily gasped at the mention of the Dreadling lord. Princess Demetra looked shocked.

"If this is true, why does she look like the Ruby Princess?" King Regal demanded.

"Because Rudgrin is wearing a mask," Roxanne replied.

"Guards!" Rudgrin shrieked. "Arrest her." She pointed at Roxanne. "*She's* the impostor."

Roxanne put both hands on her hips. "*You* are a *liar.*"

"Oh dear," Queen Gemma cried. "What are we going to do?" She turned to Rudgrin. "This young lady certainly *looks* like Roxanne."

Then the queen faced Roxanne. "But this girl, with the torn dress and messy hair, *acts* like Roxanne."

Gallivant stepped forward. "There is only one way to find out who is the true Ruby Princess."

"How?" King Regal asked.

Gallivant fixed his stern gaze on Roxanne and Rudgrin. "Which of you bears the sign?"

"Sign?" Rudgrin repeated. "What sign?"

"The mark of the Jewel Princess," Gallivant boomed. "It is something every princess is born with."

Roxanne smiled first at her cousins and then at the wizard.

"I bear the mark," she said, stepping forward.

She raised her right arm and carefully turned back the cuff of her sleeve. There, for all the world to see, was a ruby tear-drop on her wrist.

"The birthmark in the shape of her ruby!" Gallivant declared. "She who bears the mark will wear the crown."

Then Emily, Demetra, and Sabrina raised their wrists. They, too, had a mark in the shape of their jewel.

Suddenly, their crowns began to gleam.

"Look!" a lady-in-waiting gasped. "The jewels! They're glowing."

Pip, who had been hiding behind Roxanne, fluttered to Rudgrin. "You fake! Take off your mask."

"Noooo!" howled Rudgrin as Pip peeled the mask off her face with his beak.

The court gasped when her face was revealed. She had the same blank eyes and face as the Dreadlings and looked nothing like Roxanne.

In the blink of an eye, Rudgrin was whisked out of the throne room by the palace guards. And Roxanne was ushered to the king and queen.

"I am so sorry," Roxanne said, hugging the queen tightly. "I nearly ruined everything."

Queen Gemma smoothed Roxanne's hair. "We're just glad to know you're safe."

Roxanne took her place beside her cousins. Sabrina blew her a kiss. Demetra squeezed her hand. "Welcome back," Emily whispered.

Now it was time for Roxanne to be crowned.

King Regal nodded to Gallivant, who signaled the court musicians.

Beautiful music filled the air.

Gallivant turned to the crowd. "The people of the Red Mountains have chosen one of their own to place the Ruby Crown on Princess Roxanne's head. Will he please come forward?"

There was a loud flapping, and the room was filled with smoke.

Gallivant announced, "May I present—"

"Happy!" Roxanne cried with glee. Ignoring

all royal manners, she raced to greet her friend. "It's you!"

Hapgood folded his wings and bowed low. "Greetings, Princess Roxanne of the Red Mountains." He winked and added, "And the Rushing River."

Roxanne wrapped her arms around his neck and whispered, "You must have known who I was all along."

"Yes," Hapgood confessed sheepishly. "I did. When you ran away, Gallivant gave me the shield and sent me to find you."

Gallivant then presented the Ruby Crown to Hapgood. The dragon raised it above Roxanne's head.

"Wait!" Roxanne cried. "I would like the man who forged this beautiful crown to be by my side." She searched the room for the bearded gnome.

Applesap and Marigold stood at the back of the hall with Pip, looking very embarrassed.

"Come join the celebration," Roxanne cried to all of them.

Marigold, Applesap, and Pip approached the throne.

Then Hapgood set the glittering Ruby Crown on Roxanne's head. "From this moment on, I vow to be your friend and protector for all the days of my life."

Tears of joy shone in Roxanne's eyes. She hugged and kissed each of the other princesses.

Then the Ruby Princess turned to face the court. "As the ruler of the Red Mountains, I vow to have a keen ear and a kind heart, that I might always be a loving and giving . . . friend."

Read the next sparkling adventure in
the Jewel Kingdom series!

Jewel Kingdom

The Sapphire Princess
Meets a Monster

Turn the page for a special sneak peek!

1

THE GOLDEN GIFT

"It's a perfect day for a picnic!" Princess Sabrina said as she sailed across the water in Blue Lake. She was riding in her laurel-leaf boat.

Gurt the gilliwag sat behind her, paddling the boat. The green froglike creature was a close friend of the Sapphire Princess's.

"Princess Sabrina," Gurt said in his deep voice, "this very golden afternoon matches your golden gift."

That morning a golden basket had very mysteriously arrived at the gates of the Sapphire Palace. A card was pinned to the basket. It read, *To the Sapphire Princess. Signed, A Secret Admirer.*

The golden basket was filled with bread, cheese, and chocolate. Each piece was wrapped in gold cloth and tied with a sapphire-blue ribbon.

Princess Sabrina loved the basket. She had invited her three cousins to join her for a picnic that afternoon. Demetra, the Diamond Princess, and Emily, the Emerald Princess, had arrived. While they waited for the Ruby Princess, the three cousins sailed across the lake to Bluebonnet Falls.

"Let's have a race!" Sabrina called to the Emerald Princess. Emily was on her knees, paddling a large green lily pad.

"I'm ready when you are," Princess Emily said as she pulled up next to Sabrina. "Just say the word."

Of the four Jewel Princesses, Emily was the most athletic. She ruled the Greenwood and spent her days climbing tall trees and riding through her lush green forest.

The Diamond Princess steered her boat made of white gardenias between her two cousins. Demetra ruled the White Winterland, and everything she wore was glittering white.

"I think we should wait for Roxanne," Demetra advised. "Wasn't she going to join us?"

"Roxanne is *always* late," Emily said with a frown. "If we wait for her, it will be sundown before we get to eat."

Sabrina focused her dark brown eyes on the shore. There was no sign of the Ruby Princess.

"I agree with Emily," Sabrina announced. "Let's have a race ourselves."

"No, no, no!" squeaked a yellow-and-pink butterfly as she landed on Sabrina's finger. It was Zazz, Princess Sabrina's palace adviser and best friend.

"Princess, if you race in this boat, you'll lose," Zazz sputtered. "Or sink. Just look at what we're carrying. Gurt. That heavy gold basket. The napkins and tablecloths, and all of the royal china."

Sabrina put her face nose-to-nose with the tiny butterfly. "Then I'll just have to get another boat. Any idea where I might find one?"

Blue Lake was dotted with boats. "I'll call the nymphs," Zazz said as she fluttered off the princess's finger. "They'll bring a leaf boat right over."

"Don't do that," Emily called. "Sabrina, hop on my lily pad. We'll race Demetra together."

Sabrina stood up to leap onto Emily's boat, but something tugged at her arm.

Sabrina spun around. No one was there. Just Gurt the gilliwag calmly paddling away. She looked down at the mysterious golden basket. It glittered in the afternoon sun.

"Come on, Sabrina!" Emily cried. "Jump!"

Before Sabrina could make a move, the basket danced across the bottom of the boat and leaped into her hands.

Emily gasped. "Did you see that?" she asked Demetra.

"I don't like this," Demetra said, shaking her shiny black hair. "Sabrina, you should leave that basket alone. You don't know where it came from."

"Don't be such a worrywart!" Sabrina stared

at the golden basket. "This is a present. A very magical present from a secret admirer. Full of wonderful food."

"And I'm starving," Zazz called from her perch on the boat's bow.

"Me too." Sabrina leaned forward and whispered to the butterfly, "Zazz, let's not wait until we get to Bluebonnet Falls. Why don't you and I take a piece of chocolate from the picnic basket right now?"

Zazz rubbed her little legs together. "I like chocolate. Yes, yes!"

Sabrina opened the basket. But just as her fingers touched the food, something jolted the boat.

"Whoa!" Zazz fell backward onto the floor of the boat and bent one antenna. "What was that?"

"I'm not sure!" Sabrina replied.

Thunk! Something hit the boat again.

"I'm afraid something is trying to sink us," Gurt declared, pulling his paddle into the boat.

"The water sprites must be playing a joke." Sabrina peered into the water, looking for the ghostly outline of the little sprites.

"If the sprites don't want you to see them, Princess, you won't," Zazz said as she tried to straighten her antenna.

"I'll try calling them." Sabrina cupped her hands around her mouth. "Hello? Anybody there?"

Nothing.

The Sapphire Princess leaned over the side of the boat. She was so close, her nose nearly touched the lake.

All at once two huge yellow eyes appeared just below the surface.

ABOUT THE AUTHORS

JAHNNA N. MALCOLM stands for Jahnna "and" Malcolm. Jahnna Beecham and Malcolm Hillgartner are married and write together. They have written over a hundred books for kids. Jahnna and Malcolm have written books and musicals about ballerinas, horses, ghosts, singing cowgirls, and magic.

Before Jahnna and Malcolm wrote books, they were actors. They met on the stage where Malcolm was playing a prince. And they were married on the stage where Jahnna was playing a princess.

Now they have their own prince and princess: Dash and Skye, who are almost grown up. They live in Oregon with their golden retriever, Archie.

If you want to learn more about them and hear songs from their musicals, including "The Best Christmas Pageant Ever: The Musical," visit jahnnanmalcolm.com.

Princess Tabby is no scaredy-cat!

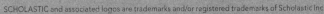

Who says princesses have to be perfect?

Join Princess Rosie and Cleo the Kitten as they go on fun adventures around Petrovia!

■SCHOLASTIC

scholastic.com

PUPPYPRINCESS

Oh my glaciers, Diary!

Princess Lina is the *coolest* girl in school!